Chapter 1

MIDDLE CHILD SYNDROME

G rowing up in a large family is both a blessing and a curse. I grew up in a very large family of sixteen, eight brothers and eight sisters. My father, Hugo, and my mother, Daniela, were amazing role models. My father spent most of his life without a mom. He was only seven or eight years old when she died, so he grew up with his father and his only brother. My mother had both parents; they were traditional or old-fashioned, Catholic, and very strict. My brothers from oldest to youngest were Guadalupe, Tobias, Simon, Ernesto, Santiago (Chago), Benjamin, Juan, and Valentin. My sisters from oldest to youngest were Josefina, Malena, Laura, Emma, Alma, Camila, and Magdalena. I, Julieta, was the youngest from the girls.

For the most part it was cool; however, as does happen in large families, not everyone feels like they belong and you become overlooked often in the most critical times. I do not regret growing up in a household full of challenging matters because it shaped me into a better, braver, and stronger individual. There were many days I felt right at home, but there also were those days I wished I had been the only child—highly unlikely because at this point in time Hispanic families had large families. I felt invisible because I could disappear for hours and no one would look for me, or even know I was gone. I felt nonexistent.

I was number eleven of the living children. I had five younger brothers, and that is why I found it was easier to speak with guys; guys were less critical and had less drama going on in their lives. So I did boy things while growing up. I talked about and played with cars, played with marbles, and watched football games with my younger brothers. To me that was normal because my older sisters were into boys, and at that point we had nothing in common. The feeling of inattention or neglect is known as the middle child syndrome. It *does* exist, folks. This is a syndrome where middle children feel excluded because the first child may receive more privileges and/or responsibilities and the younger child is more likely to get pampered (Wikipedia, 2017). Middle children often are ignored (or at least we feel that way). It was quite difficult to get noticed among fifteen other siblings. There were so many of us competing for the same attention that, at the end of the day, I was satisfied with having my father and mother, a shared bed, and warm food to come home to every day. For me, that was awesome!

As long as you were a well-behaved child, who was doing well in all your classes, did not have teachers calling your parents, and stayed out of any type of trouble like doing drugs, smoking, and/or drinking, you were pretty much an invisible child. This was acceptable, that is, until you hit the teenage years when you turned to friends instead of family. Friends become your number one go-to

BULLIES CREATE BULLIES

NATI CARRILLO

for advise and reassurance. There is longing for acceptance among peers that only friends can fulfill during this stage in life. Unfortunately, we often find friends who are unhealthy, ruthless, or bullies, yet we stand by them and start to make bad choices. Those choices, better known as freewill, become a lifetime of struggles and disappointments. So take it from someone who has made her share of mistakes in life, you have to love yourself first to love others. You have to have an idea where you want to be in life and what you want to do in life, write it down, look at it every week or month, and do this over and over again. Research says *you accomplish 50 % of what you write down.*

Life is a journey. That journey is not always a smooth one, and life teaches us lessons. We take those lessons to another level. We learn from them, from our mistakes, and hopefully we do not repeat them. Know that there *is* a stage in your life, such as the teenage years, when you start craving love, nurturing, and attention from friends. At this point in life you are vulnerable, and you might be confused and develop unhealthy lifetime relationships that only lead you to a path of destruction.

Listen to your parents when they offer you advice. They know what you are going through, believe it or not. They have lived and learned from their lives, and made similar choices or similar mistakes, so they are able to tell you what works and what does not. When your parents repeatedly tell you that a person "is not good for you," he or she is probably someone you should stay away from. *You* as the obedient child, however, believe your parents just want you to be miserable and miss out on life. So you choose the contrary; you do your own thing, and yes, that decision will either ruin you or make you a better person. What choices are you likely to make? What and who is going to define you?

Chapter 2

DEATH AND DISAPPOINTMENT

Mom and Dad lost their first ten male babies due either to miscarriage or neural tube defects. So, in desperation and growing faith, they made a promise to God and our Virgin Mary that if the next baby were spared, they would name him or her Guadalupe after *La Virgin de Guadalupe*. Our family believed and was grounded in Catholic principles. We grew up in a traditional environment where a marriage is between a man and woman with the purpose of multiplying, and if you happened to get married, your marriage was for a lifetime. Divorce was never mentioned; it was never the option to any problem. When you married, you married for life, and that was it, no questions asked. That was our way of living, our way of thinking, and our understanding of marriage.

Sometimes I still find myself asking repeatedly, "How did Hugo and Daniela raise so many children and remain sane and faithful to each other?" With God and a mutual understanding that marriage, and life itself, is based on a give-and-take relationship, they accomplished raising six-teen children—no twins, all single births. It was evident that it was difficult for them since Dad was the only breadwin-ner and Mom a housewife, but they managed to surpass it all. I am still speechless today. Not a day goes by that I wonder how they held it all together. They had their share of ups and downs, and death and life experiences, but they obviously had a relationship of understanding toward each other that surpassed all their struggles.

Growing up, and even as teenagers, we go through a dif-ferent set of behaviors just to get that much-needed atten-tion. We do things that normally we would not do at home, but we do it to feel wanted, to be included, and to be part of something. Even if we know deep down in our gut it is wrong and bad for us, we still do it! We know this, but we remain true to our new friends just to fit in, be noticed, and be someone. We act like someone different to the person when we are at home in the company of our parents. We disregard all the rules our parents taught us and make room for new and exciting things because we are invincible, be-cause we can do it (or so we think) with no consequences, and because we belong to a group. "How awesome is that?" In this book you will go on a journey with the author to learn how simple and/or not-so-simple mistakes affect others in our life. Unfortunately, sometimes those who make the mis-takes do not realize the turmoil that is unleashed with one bad choice.

Some events I write about may not be what my elders or others know to be true, but they are *my* perceptions at the lowest and highest points in my life.

Indeed, it was one hot day, when I was about three or four years old, I had on a pretty blue dress that I loved to wear on Sundays. It was slightly stained, but I was happy to wear it. My sandals kept slipping off; they were hand-me-downs from my older sisters; with seven older sisters, I had a lot of hand-me-downs. I do not think I ever complained once about getting hand-me-down shoes. I was still happy to wear them because to me they were new. My hair was a bit knotted, and my face and fingers were still sticky from the waffles I had eaten earlier, but I was content wearing my favorite dress.

Why was I dressed in my Sunday best if it was not Sunday? We were not in church; we were jam-packed in a small room. I remember almost everyone was crying. There seemed to be so much pain and sadness in the room, except for me. "¿Qué pasa padre, por qué estás llorando?" ("What's wrong dad, why are you crying?") He looked down at me sadly and said, "Tu hermanita se fue con Dios; se dormio." ("Your sister has gone with God, she went to sleep.") I was not quite understanding what he said so, I headed toward the front of the room where Mom had been kneeling for a long time. There in the far corner lay a white coffin, a tiny coffin surrounded with such beautiful decorations, fresh roses and carnations. Oh, what a sight! What was this? As I was going down the hall, I could not help notice that every-one was wearing black veils and black clothes. When I came up behind Mom, she immediately got up and grabbed my hand so I would go back to the bench, but I forced myself out of her grip. She was not crying, but her face was puffy, her eyes were red, and her nose looked like she had been rubbing it for a long time. Her face had a blank stare; she looked dazed. I think she was praying. My brothers and sisters were crying, and Dad, holding his white handkerchief, kept blowing his nose every five minutes. It was a scary sight that I will never forget.

As I got closer, I noticed a small baby in the coffin; it was my little sister, Ariana, who just days earlier had been born. She was so small, so lovely. I touched her, and she felt cold; I touched her again. I tried to wake her up but nothing; she was lifeless, cold as ice, with no movement. Tears ran down my face. She looked so innocent like an angel. It could not be Ariana, who I was going to play with, teach, and protect. That is what big sisters are supposed to do. I cried for a long time but returned to the bench where I just stared at her. Quería preguntarle a mi padre, "¿Por qué?" ¿Por qué le había pasado esto? (I wanted to ask my Father, why had this happened to her?") She was a baby! I could not bring myself to ask him. He was too sad, so I knew I had to keep quiet and just sit there and wait. She was a baby, twenty-one days old; she had her whole life ahead of her. I had no words to console Father. Mom, on the other hand, seemed calmer, praying, and to me it seemed she was doing better than Dad.

Chapter 3

GREAT DISAPPOINTMENTS

F irmly holding Father's hand, I remember practically skipping to my first day of school or registration. I felt the butterflies, my nerves. I was excited, but soon that excitement became disappointment. It was prekindergarten registration, and as luck would have it, my *age* did not work in my favor that year. Although I was ready, the lady kept telling Father, "She is not ready." The lady asked for my birth date—September 7, 1971—and then looked bothered as she returned all Father's forms and advised him to come back next year. I was a late baby.

What the heck was a late baby? I did not know you had to plan the birth of your child to match the school years (remember, there were sixteen of us). Well, that did it. I started to cry. Poor Father, he tried his best, and now furious, he started yelling at the lady."¿Cómo no puedes aceptarla, está llorando, quería comenzar la escuela, ella está lista." ("How can you not accept her, she is crying, she wanted to start school, she is ready.") The lady apologized and tried to explain the rules to us. My father, being impatient, preferred not to listen and walked off, mumbling all sorts of bad words regarding how he felt about the rules. As we walked away, I looked back at the school, sighed, and sobbed some more. I cried all the way home until Father told me to stop and reassured me, "Mira tienes mas tiempo para hugar en casa," that I had more time to play at home. I stopped crying not because I did not want to go to school but because I saw he was not angry anymore.

Finally, that day came. I was five years old and ready with Father to register. Again Father was the only one taking us to register because Mom had a lot of household chores and had to care for the rest of us at home. I was finally in school; I was so looking forward to seeing other kids my age—not older than me but *my* age. You get tired of seeing your brothers and sisters all day, every day. It was time to make new friends, play in the school's playground, and finally bring books home like my older brothers and sisters did. Boy, I was excited!

I craved attention! I was not going to be that shy girl no one noticed at home. One of my first good experiences in prekindergarten was winning first place in a competition. The competition had to do with drawing a picture of a favorite person/cartoon. I drew the Incredible Hulk; he was my favorite character growing up. I had fun drawing him too. I drew him as he looked on TV: a big green man with messy hair, huge muscles, and torn shirt and pants because he outgrew his clothes when he turned into the Hulk. Lacking confidence, I was sure I had no chance of winning. I drew him just for fun.

The day finally came to announce the winners. They were only going to announce the first three places. Once they announced the third and second places, I continued playing. I knew that was it; I had not won. There was no way on earth I would win first, and it was okay not to win; I would be okay with that too. Someone shouted, "Julieta, they called your name; You won!" I was stunned, speechless, and immobile for a couple of minutes. Then I stood and sat back down; I did not know what to do! I kept thinking that I drew the Incredible Hulk only for fun, and there was no way I could have won first place. They repeated the first-place winner's name. "I won!" The announcer told the winners to come to the office to claim their prizes. It was then that all the students in the class, including the teacher, started screaming and pulling me toward the door. I could not believe it! They did say my name! What for me had been a fun game became my first accomplishment where I became somebody. I was no longer invisible. I had been noticed in front of the whole school. Wow, it felt great!

As I walked to the office, my legs started wobbling, my hands were shaking and sweaty, and my thoughts were racing. "I won, I really won!" I will claim whatever prize I am getting!" So I walked into the office and gave them my name, and they congratulated and hugged me for my excellent drawing of the Hulk. I did not want to blurt out, "Okay, where is my prize," but that is what I was thinking. The commotion lasted awhile and then settled when the announcer gave me a nicely wrapped box with a huge red bow. As I started walking back to the classroom, I wanted to stop and unwrap it, but I couldn't bring myself to undo such pretty wrapping, and I wanted my family to see me open it and see what I had won. As I walked, I kept asking myself, "What could it be; What could it be?" When I opened the door to the classroom, I was nearly tackled by the whole class.

They kept asking, "What is it, what is it?" I replied, "I don't know, I don't want to open it yet!" That was the first time I had been influenced by my peers to do something I did not want to do, but at the same time, I felt I had to open it or I would have everyone against me—and that feeling was much worse to bear. I did not like it.

My group and the whole class kept staring at me and my present, giving me ugly looks because I would not open it. Peer pressure—it is real people. So yes, I was emotionally forced to open the gift and share this moment with my class; eventhough, I felt I needed to share it with my family first. The minute I started removing the bow, everyone got around me and started ripping at it. I was yelling, "Wait, wait, I want to do it; it's mine; Stop, please stop!" No one listened, and pretty soon there they were, a set of beautiful shiny books. Wow! I kept trying to see them, but everyone was trying to grab them, and then they started throwing them to each other.

Once the whole class could see they were books, they started laughing. "Books, they gave you books! "You don't even know how to read yet." Laughter broke out. The teacher asked firmly for everyone to return to his or her desk. I kept asking myself, "Why did they laugh; What was wrong with my books?" I loved them. I did not know how to read, but I knew I was going to learn! I did not want to cry in front of everyone so I ran out to the bathroom. As soon as I opened the door, I broke out sobbing. Tears ran down my face. I was so disappointed. A feeling of sadness came over me, and I started to question myself. "Do I even want to go home with books as a present; Maybe my family will laugh too, and then I will get this ugly feeling again." I did not understand my class's reaction at all. I won fair and square, and no one seemed to care. I walked slowly back to class, trying to contain my tears, wiping them away. I walked in and, with a firm look, stared at everyone with disappointment. Then I just sat down and stared at my desk. They knew I was mad for no one laughed, no one stared back, and no one made a sound. That ruined my whole day. Kids can be cruel.

Chapter 4

LOST AND FOUND

Father would help Mom early in the mornings. He would comb and braid all the girls' hair for school. He would pull so hard to make a perfect braid that my eyes looked like they were getting pulled with the hair. It hurt, so to relieve some pain I would hold my eyes forward with my hands while he braided my hair. That helped. Mother would make fresh tortillas and breakfast every morning. We were always running late because someone was either holding up the bathroom or the shower, so we rarely ate at home. We each got a chorizo and egg taco on a flour tortilla, dropping some of it, as we ran to catch the bus. The bus driver possibly did not like us because we would leave crumbs on the bus nearly every day.

There were about twelve to thirteen of us getting on the bus at the same time so we were lucky if we found a seat; we stood most of the time. The entire bus smelled of homemade tacos, but we ate as if we had no care in the world. I think we were grateful to at least have some food on our table. We saw how exhausted Father looked day in and day out, trying to give us the best. We did not care what others thought or said about us; we ate with gratitude. We were an old-fashioned, simple, and humble family.

In kindergarten I found myself sitting in a classroom that was not my homeroom (I thought was mine on the first day of school). The teacher called out everyone's name but mine, and I started to panic. My cheeks flushed, my hands got sweaty, and my heart started racing. Once roll call was done, the teacher asked if everyone's name had been called. If not, we were to raise our hands. So, I slowly raised my hand, and everyone turned to look at me. The teacher asked for my name, and I softly said, "Julieta." She checked her roster and said, "No, your name is not here." She had someone take me to the office to get my class schedule. I was so embarrassed about being taken to the office. "Why didn't I remember my classroom number or the name of my teacher?" I thought. The office sent me to the right classroom with a huge white name tag around my neck. It showed the classroom number and the teacher's name, but the sign covered my entire chest. I felt like a lost dog with a name tag around its neck. As I walked into class, everyone stared again. The teacher was told, "This one belongs to you; she was lost." I heard giggles in the back of the room. I turned in frustration to see who it was, but no one laughed anymore.

After that humiliating day, I was going to make sure I knew where I was supposed to be. In order to do that, I walked back and forth around the school until I could find my way to my homeroom several times. The next morning after attendance was called, another little girl came in with the office personnel who said, "This one belongs to you; she was lost too." A few giggles erupted, and I turned back and gave those same girls an ugly stare; they stopped giggling. I knew then that this new girl and I were going to be good friends. We were the lost ones, so technically we needed to find each other. Why is it okay for kids to laugh at other kids' mishaps and continue as if it is normal, expected behavior? The teacher did not point out that teasing or laughing was not welcomed behavior. Someone needs to change that. Teachers should hold students accountable to know it is not okay to laugh at others' mistakes.

We were all waiting for the bell to ring for the next class to start as we did every day after lunch. Everyone was sitting and leaning against the wall except my new friend, Ava, and me. They had left a space for us to sit, and everyone kept staring at us, so we looked at each other and sat down. As we sat down, the class broke out in laughter. Again I wondered, "What the heck are they laughing at now?" Soon the bell rang, but no one got up, which was odd. So we got up, but something pulled me back. I had a huge wad of gum stuck to the bottom of my pants. Aha, now it made complete sense why no one stood before we did. They wanted to make sure they saw our reactions to their stupid joke, which ruined my pants. I was furious and annoyed. I told the teacher what happened, but everyone denied doing anything. This keeps proving that kids, no matter what grade, can be callous and unkind to each other—and for what?

For the rest of the day, I tried to fabricate a story to explain to my parents why I was coming home wearing someone else's clothes. The school nurse had loaned me a pair of pants to wear. My father, the one person who could protect me, was too busy with work because we needed the money and could not afford to take time off. Still, he felt bad for me, so bad that he asked me, "Si quieres que deje de trabajar para aver que castigo se puede hacer, lo haré, pero tú dime" ("If you want me to take off work to see what can be done, I will, just let me know what you want me to do.") The fact he asked for my opinion at all made me feel important. I wanted to act grown up, so I let it go. I was not willing to have Father take a day off work because, God knows, we needed the money. I sucked it up and pretended to be okay for the benefit of the entire family. With so many mouths to feed, one day off work would impact all of us, not just me, so I said to him, "No apa, yo puedo areglar algo, gracias." ("No Dad, I will see what I can do, thank you anyway.") I was okay, and I could handle it. Just the fact that Father was at a disadvantage because he couldn't leave work added to the problem of bullies getting away with that behavior. So many kids will give up, while others become bullies or join the pack because if they do not, they might end up being the one bullied. I guess if you cannot beat them, you join them, right? No, that is not the answer. So what do you do?

I think students should receive a class on bullies and bullying to increase awareness of this critical issue that is causing some young teens to commit suicide. Are you a bully, have been a bully, or know someone being bullied? What is a bully? A bully is defined by the website Wikipedia as any person who uses strength or power to harm or intimidate those who are weaker. The synonyms for *bully* include tormentor, oppressor, despot, tyrant, teaser, mocker, joker, aggressor, persecutor, intimidator, dictator, and harasser. It is also important to know the definition of *harasser*, which is someone who annoys, pesters, stalks, hounds, or bothers.

It was interesting to find out that certain people I know fall into one or more categories of bullying. I fell into two categories of being a bully in second grade, and I have dealt with bullies up until recently. I think it has become so much a normal part of living that some people do not realize when they are doing it or simply do not care, but know that most people who bully you are people who envy you, loathe your success, and yes, sometimes might even like or love you. We need to teach people how *not* to accept a bully's behavior, and it has to start at home. Parents need to build trust and time, and have a plan for their children if they encounter bullies.

I still very much enjoyed school, studying, and doing homework in kindergarten, but I grew to hate nap time. During nap time, some kids took advantage of those who were sleeping, often stealing stuff from them. So you could not go to sleep; if you did, you were a target. Most teachers declare that bullying is a case of kids being kids. But, no, it is children learning that bad behaviors go unchanged and even unpunished. Bullies feel a sense of power because they are in control of someone else's feelings and actions, or it could be that at home they are the ones getting bullied.

Competition, can be an intimidating word for a lot of people, but for me, it was a time to have fun. I loved competing in dance contests because it was my time to shine. I enjoyed practicing, dancing, and being around my friends so much that I did not see winning as a contest but as a group get-together. We were having fun doing what I loved to do: dance. Our group consisted of about nine girls. Faustina was the leader, and her mother helped us plan the dress attire that would look great when we competed. She was an awesome lady and friend; all the girls loved to be around her. She helped us train and prepare for the dance competition at the Performing Arts Center. We dressed '50s style with red handkerchiefs around our necks, white shirts, plaid skirts, lacy socks, and old-fashioned shoes. We danced to "Rock Around the Clock," and we looked and played the part well! We won first place! This was yet another time I was noticed. What a feeling; it was a thrilling experience for all of us! Do not ask about my grades, but I know I was passing; otherwise, Father would have been called. He was so busy that I signed my own report cards (as most of you do too), and no one questioned anything, so my grades were good.

Chapter 5

BULLIES MAKING BULLIES

S till timid and fearful about gaining new friends, my social circle was quite small. I had one friend and what seemed like many enemies. On more than one occasion, my friend, Ava, and I would just hang around the playground, and it was not long before this one guy named Aaron started to bother us. He started with small talk, and then he started teasing us, picking up dirt and throwing it at us. Then he started kicking us, but he mostly kicked and shouted at me. He actually kicked my lower front legs, and while doing that he shouted, "Ha-ha, I got you!" He irritated the hell out of me! I kept shouting at him to stop, but he never did; he acted this way almost to the end of the school year.

Two weeks before classes were out, his friend came up to me and said Aaron liked me and wanted to know if I would be his girlfriend. I stopped. I was so confused. All year this pesky little kid nagged the hell out of me and bullied me, all because he liked me! I did not understand. I yelled at his friend, "Tell him of course not; I do not want to be his girlfriend; I do not like him." "He hurt me." I could not understand his attitude. I thought, how could someone claim to like you and be cruel to you at the same time? That was messed up! In the days following that confrontation Aaron knew I disliked him, so he did not attempt to speak to me. That was totally fine with me. I sure the hell did not miss his teasing, kicking, and shouting.

A vast part of me hated first grade, and the other part of me just wanted to stay home. "Why, why, did I want to stay at home?" Maybe it was just to avoid people altogether. I kept thinking back to Aaron because despite his bad behavior, I was angry that he did not know how to show his feelings. He should have known the kicking and harassing me was not a healthy relationship, and if anything, it was taking away from something that could have been. I figured he may have been having a difficult time in his life at home too, but he never made an effort to hold a real conversation with me. I do not remember ever having a true friend in first grade to confide in, and home felt no different. I knew Mom had too much on her plate to worry about, so she did not have time for me and my childish stories. Dad was at work all the time, and my brothers and sisters were in school all day with their own problems. I had no one to gossip with or question about stuff going on in my life. Even though I had a huge family, I felt lonely and sad, and I grew angry about everything and toward everyone. I felt the anger, frustration, and desperation accumulating inside me.

Chapter 6

SHAMED

Walking out of the lunch hall, I noticed someone I had not seen in school before, someone very different. This was my first occurrence of culture shock. Jonah, who was sitting and eating on the curbside, looked like he had been enjoying his lunch. I came up behind him, grabbed his sandwich out of his hands, took the cheese puffs out of his lunch box, and began eating them. He looked back and stood up in fear. His face saddened as he saw me, his shoulders fell slightly forward, and slowly but surely he sat back down. He never made eye contact after that.

He was a white boy, whiter than me, and I thought I was whiter than most. He drew my attention right away; he had been sitting alone. He had light brown to reddish straight hair that fell somewhat over his eyes for I could not see his entire face. He was thin and scrawny, timid looking, and he was wearing a nicely ironed, white-collared shirt, nice dark blue slacks, and awesome shoes. "Could I have been jealous that he looked that good?" I may have been. He looked too good to be sitting alone. I may have thought he was cute, but there was nothing to justify my horrible behavior toward him.

I guess I was starting to forget how alone and invisible I had been, and those years of being bullied were rubbing off—yes, an excuse for my behavior. Mind you, I was alone too. I do not remember if my friend was absent due to sickness or other reasons, but, yes, I was alone. There was no one to advise me to stop and/or no one to see this unacceptable behavior, which I had been subjected to in earlier years. I could not grasp why he was sitting alone; he had no friends and seemed to be okay with it. I do not know why, but in the following days the stealing of his food during lunchtime became a routine of mine. He was alone, I was alone, and being mean to him was the only way I felt important, even though it was for a short while. I think he was afraid of me. Thank God I stopped sometime later. I do not remember what happened to him and did not give him much time or thought to find out. I just hope I was not an awful nightmare he continues having today. If ever I see him again, I will apologize. He did not deserve to be bullied; he was probably a great person that I never got to know personally.

This was a time in my life that I am *not* proud of and hate to acknowledge, but it did happen. I hope others learn that being a bully stems from having been a bullied *victim* at some point in their lives. Fragile-looking, innocent—that was Jonah, and that was me too. "Are we targets just because of our appearance?" Many would say yes. "There was no power, no fame, and no reward for being a bully to Jonah, so why did I do it?" I do not have the answer, but some of this awful behavior might have had something to do with what was happening to me at home. I knew my behavior was wrong. We lived by strict church rules/teachings at home. My parents never taught me to do that, and we lived by the Golden Rule: "Do unto others as you would have them do unto you." That was not what I was practicing in the second grade, shameful to say.

What was happening to me that would cause me to act so selfishly toward someone of the opposite sex? Well, part of the middle children stigma is that you're forgotten or neglected, and as the eleventh child, I was pretty much invisible to almost everyone except Grandpa. Any attention was good, right? Wrong, his attention was definitely messed up at so many levels. I loved my grandfather dearly, that is, until he made me feel dirty. My sisters and I would gather round Grandpa to listen to his old stories. While doing this, he would sit us in his lap—first one of us, then two, and sometimes he had up to three of us at once in his lap. It was fun at first; then things started to happen that no child should ever experience at any age, with anyone.

We did not know it was wrong until years later, believe it or not, as grown women. Grandpa, may he rest in peace, was rarely mentioned, especially at the girls' get-togethers. But one time someone raised the question, "Did Grandpa ever touch you?" We all stared at each other as if we already knew the answer, but were too afraid to admit to or even speak about it. No one said a word for what seemed a long time. There was a mutual silence, a few tears, and a few sniffles. Then I said, "He made me feel very uncomfortable when he sat me in his lap." "He would start singing a song and then out of nowhere squeeze my nipples, he would inappropriately touch me." (I was only eight years old at the time.) And he burst out in laughter as he did it! I tried to pull away and get away from him, but I could not. He was too strong. "Did anyone of you have similar experiences?" I felt ashamed. "Was it only me who experienced this?" Everyone else seemed to be laughing and enjoying his company. I thought I was the only one feeling that way.

Then my other sisters, one by one, said they too felt uneasy around him. I became very upset at my sisters for not telling me, not warning me about him. I was the smallest; I felt they should have protected me. "Why didn't any of you say or do anything about him or his behavior? Why?" Tears poured from my eyes. My sister sitting next to me hugged me tightly, and we cried and spent what seemed like hours comforting each other.

"How many of us did he do this to; What about our nieces, your baby girls?" "How do we know he did not do this to them too," I asked. "We have to forgive him, Sis" were the only words that came out of my older sister's mouth. What? How could we? It was wrong, evil, to do this to anyone! My father never found out about his father's actions. Father is eighty-three years old now, and at this point in his life with cancer in remission, he does not need to live the rest of his time living in regret or hate. That would be unhealthy. Father was working all the time, so there was no way he would have found out without someone telling him, and Mother was too busy with chores. She thought he was a great person—we all did! We cried, still wondering, "He loved us, right?" It felt good to know that we were all in the same boat, highly ignorant and feeling guilty for not doing or saying anything to anyone. We had no one to blame, but we knew each other's pain. We had a mutual understanding not to mention this to Father, ever. Grandfather had passed so there was no need to stress Father about his behavior. There would be nothing for him to do except feel responsible and hate his father.

These events may have prevented us from being more engaging with our husbands and more confident in our marriages, but it is what it is. How can you get help for something you did not know was wrong in the first place or, better yet, when everyone around you acts like it was a normal part of life. We had no choice but to accept this way of living because we were too afraid to speak up. Never be those parents who either look too busy or appear so unapproachable that your own kids cannot confide in you. Those we love the most hurt us the most. We loved Grandpa; he was fun, but we learned to be silent, accept his behavior, and put it all behind us because none of us were brave enough to speak up. Do not be that person. Speak up! Chances are someone else is going through the same thing you are.

Chapter 7

THE GOOD, THE BAD, AND THE HOSPITAL

When third grade came along, I was and looked more like a boy. I loved to play with marbles, and I really enjoyed hanging around with the boys in school. I think I preferred to be with boys because I had five younger brothers at home with whom I hung out and played marbles, among other things. Boys were less critical of me. I did not have to worry about putting on makeup as I did in the second grade. Of course, I removed it before getting home because Mother or Father would have slapped me if they caught me putting on makeup.

There was only one other girl in the third grade who liked playing too, but she was not as good as I was, or so I thought. I enjoyed playing marbles so much that I gathered enough to fill an empty gallon-size milk bottle. I was better than most guys at playing marbles; I was a legit pro! I stopped playing after I got in trouble for accusing another girl in my class of stealing my marbles; I did catch her red-handed though. She was stealing my marbles during lunch break, but she denied it. I had no proof, so I was being disrespectful for that allegation. Rather than make a big deal of it, I stopped playing and gave the marbles to my brothers at home. That was that; I never played after that incident.

Aside from the game of marbles, I loved mathematics. It was my favorite subject. The teacher had us play a math game called Ring Around the World. The teacher would give us a multiplication problem if you got it wrong you have to sit but if you got it right you would continue until you reached the last chair/desk. I would get to the end of the room, so I won several times. It was fun, and the teacher would give us nice prizes. It was an awesome class, and the teacher made it interesting and so much fun. Teachers play a crucial role in a student's learning—or not learning as it happened with me in high school.

During one lunch period at school, I was having a slight pain on the right side of my back, but I did not think anything of it and kept playing. It was not until I got home that the pain seemed much worse. I felt a sharp pain with each and every breath I took. I went to the bathroom, but since we had an outhouse, it was impossible to see the color of my urine or my stool so I could not identify if something was wrong. An outhouse is a small building with one or two holes where we did our business. We were poor and could not afford an indoor toilet system. Besides, back then most people we knew had outhouses, so it was normal to us. My mother advised me to urinate in a can to see the color of my urine, and it was bright red. My lower back pain grew stronger. She gave me a homemade Kotex maxi pad and told me

I had started my period. She did not think it was a big deal. I asked her, "¿Pero duele tanto?" ("But why, does it hurt this much?")

Mother told Pa that I may have gotten a visitor: my period. So my dad went back to praying. My body started shivering and shaking uncontrollably due to a high fever, so Father handed me a Coke; Cokes were the cure for fever back then. After having a couple drinks of the soda, I started crying and holding my breath. It really hurt; the pain to my lower back was now intolerable. My dad handed me couple of Tylenol capsules for the pain and continued praying. My body started shaking again, and I was cold so they covered me. Then I started speaking nonsense, and I became confused.

Finally, they decided to take me to the closest emergency room, my father mumbling, "Esto no puede ser tú regla ("This could not be my period.") They took me in right away because my blood was getting infected. I was getting septic, which is a really bad blood infection that can be fatal. I was in so much pain and had such a high fever that they pushed some medication through my rectum for the fever. By this time, I had started to vomit so I could not hold anything down. As soon as I got to my room, several nurses came to my mother and asked all the medical questions. I remember falling in and out of sleep but was still shaking a lot.

The worse experience I had in my entire life was being a patient in a hospital. I was diagnosed with a serious kidney infection traveling to the blood. The nurses were given strict orders to decrease my fever, start intravenous fluids, and administer pain medication. It was not long before two nurses showed up in white uniforms to start an intravenous (IV) line for antibiotics. The antibiotics had to be given through the vein since the infection had traveled to the blood; this was the fastest way to stop it and avoid causing more harm to my body. I had a nurse on each side of the bed holding both my hands down. The first nurse poked me and could not find the vein, so the next nurse tried, but she could not find it either. They kept poking and sticking for a good hour; they said I had no visible veins because I was dehydrated. They grabbed me tighter and tighter until I could no longer fight them. I became tired and could not struggle with them any longer. I guess Mom got upset with me because she reached over and held me down too. I was yelling at her, "Usted no me quiere, por qué les esta ayu-dando?" ("You don't love me, why are you helping them?") I was shouting that she did not love me or else she would not help them or cause me more pain. I know now, as a mother, that I would have done the same thing if that would help my son or daughter recover. After multiple attempts, they finally found the vein and administered intravenous fluids and antibiotics several times a day.

About a half hour after starting the IV line, those two nurses came back into my room. I fearfully asked, "What now," and began to cry. I knew their presence was of no good as they started to prepare me for a shower by covering my IV line. "Are you crazy," I yelled. "I am very cold; I am freez-ing in here." The fact was my fever had spiked dangerously to 104 degrees. In order to get the fever down, my body needed cooling off fast to prevent further complicating my sickness with seizures. I called out to Mother, "¡mamá no las dejes!" ("Mom, do not let them.") My mother just sat there in complete silence, not saying a word, and let the nurses carry me to the shower kicking and screaming. Once in the shower, I noticed a tub full of ice cubes. What, ice? No way! What the heck! They lay me in that cold, ice-filled water and poured some more over me. I was shouting, kicking, and shivering all at once. This was torture. "Help, Ma, ayudeme por favor!" ("¡Ayuda, mamá, ayudeme por favor!") Mother never came into the shower with the nurses. This ordeal, for me, lasted an eternity, fifteen minutes in nurse's time. I hated the nurses, the hospital, my mother, and everyone for doing this to me.

Every day that followed was a breeze. Luckily, I didn't run high fevers after that. The antibiotics were working, and even though I was still having hematuria (blood in the urine) and dysuria (pain while urinating), I felt 50 percent better than the day before. After about seven days in the hospital, I could not stand to drink any more Sprite or 7UP; even water made me nauseous. That was all I could drink in the hospital to flush my kidneys. They did not let me have tea, coffee, or Coke, which I loved to drink at home.

Two days prior to my discharge from the hospital, I received a big poster signed by the whole class, wishing me well and hoping I had a speedy recovery. That made me feel special, and it was a great feeling to be missed. Once I left the hospital, I didn't even look back.

Chapter 8

DANCING IT UP

Performing in elementary school was a thing for me now. I participated in another talent show with a guy friend of mine, Manny. My social life in this school involved only two friends. Manny and I danced to the song "Greased Lightning." My parents and family were never invited; my dad would have killed me (not literally) if he knew I was dancing with a boy in school in front of people. In fifth grade I really wanted to join guitar or choir class, but I knew Pa did not have money to spend leisurely. So I never asked him or told him about music class. I loved listening to music, singing, and especially dancing; those were my favorite extracurricular activities.

During this time in my life, I grew very lonely and angry toward my older sister because she eloped with her boyfriend. She was only thirteen, so I felt this guy stole her from me. She met him supposedly in school, but he looked much older than a junior high student. They would meet at school, so I figured she did not go to class all the time.

I did not think her relationship was serious until she told me she was going to escape with him. I tried to convince her otherwise, but she was so much in love that she did not listen to me. She told me the day, the time, and how she was going to do it. He was supposed to pass by the house, and she would take her bags and jump into his car—just like that, that simple. Oh, but if my Father knew about it, it was not going to happen on his watch. So I told Father about her plan. Father did not sleep a wink that night; he kept watch with a beer can in one hand, and a long shiny machete in his other hand. My sister was so upset with me that she did not speak to me for couple weeks, and then she was gone. She did not tell me this time. I hated her for leaving me. She was not only my favorite sister but a friend too. Now I was truly lonely.

Camila and I did not get along because she was Mom's favorite daughter. Mother took her everywhere and left me at home. Father would tell Mother to take me, but she kept saying no, I had to stay home. For what reason, I do not know. So we were not the best company when we were left alone. I guess I liked to be mean to my sister and teased her all the time. We kept getting into physical fights, but Mom would always hit me, not her; she always assumed it was my fault.

My world was falling apart, and my only close sister and friend had eloped with her boyfriend. Father could not accept that she had gone so he searched for her day and night, only to find out she was just a block away. He found her, dragged her home, and whipped her so she would not leave again. Father did not want to give up his child. I suppose he believed she was too young to ruin her life and too young to live with a grown man. He must have brought her back more than three times until the day she gave him the news. My sister had invented a horrible story that our parents were abusing us all at home. And then she told Father she was pregnant.

Child Protective Services (CPS) came to investigate my parents and their alleged behavior. Oh was Father furious when they bombarded him with questions and accusations. He kept asking the CPS caseworker for advice on this type of situation, but she could not answer that. Father and Mother passed her awful evaluation, and not one of us was removed from home. Father was acting as a concerned parent but was advised not to spank us. He was having a tough time with people coming to his home and telling him how to raise and discipline his children, but no one offered real advice. Afterward, Father called the cops and told them he was letting my sister go with the guy because she claimed she was pregnant and he would not fight it anymore. The cops advised him not to let her go, but he disagreed and said, "No, ella está embarazada llevensela." ("She is pregnant, take her.") The cops tried to calm him down, but Father could not have her pregnant at home. He was offended, saddened, and humiliated. He had finally given up. He told the cops he only wanted what was best for all of us, and if he did not punish us, how was he supposed to teach us to be good individuals? "Entonces, ¿cómo voy a castigar a mis hijos, a enseñarles a distinguir entre el bien y el mal y a quién más les importará lo suficiente como para enseñarles? Todos ustedes están equivocados, muy equivocados"

Chapter 9

COMING OF AGE

The famous thirteen—I was finally a teenager. This was an exciting point in my life. Mother would still prefer to take Camila shopping with her and Dad instead of me. So soon I was finding entertainment elsewhere. My neighbor Mirna, who had been my eloped sister's best friend, became my friend. She would invite me to her house, and I would go after my parents left. Mirna had an older brother, Lorenzo. He was seventeen, tall, dark, and handsome, but it seemed he had a crush on my sister Alma, so I let them be. They held hands every so often, so I figured they were an item. All of us would tag along to the drive-in movies, and every chance I got, I glanced at Lorenzo to see what he and Sis were up to. I did catch him glancing back at me several times and assumed he had mixed emotions. Alma denied they were a couple. I was shocked. It did not make sense that they often held each other's hand and yet claimed not to be together.

Days later, Lorenzo approached me and asked if he could call me sometime. I asserted that Father would not allow that.

"Do you not know my father and what he is capable of if he finds out?" Lorenzo told me, "Hablo con Don Hugo, si quieres para pedirle permiso y poder hablar contigo, tú dime?" He would speak to Father and get his permission to talk to me if that was what I preferred he do. I was shocked. "What, one minute you are holding hands with my sister Alma, and the next minute you are initiating a more serious relationship with me." "I do not understand; What is it with you; What do you really want from me?" I asked. He looked straight into my eyes, held my hands, and said, "You, you are what and who I want, but I want to do things right." "Let me speak to your father about us." "If you prefer, I could bring my dad should we need help for persuasion." "I just want to be able to speak with you without worrying about what he will do if he catches us." "Do you want me to do it?" I smiled nervously. "Ah, ah, I don't know what to say. What if he gets mad and says no?" He replied, "Pues nimodo pero se hizo el esfuerzo, no?"("Well too bad but an effort was made, right?") *Wow*, I thought, this guy seemed serious, too serious, and Father was not about to negotiate with anyone. Magdalena had just eloped a couple months earlier. I was truly frightened for my neighbor and me and this whole arrangement.

I unexpectedly told him to come next week, and Lorenzo was pleased. I was terrified all week until that day came around. On that day, Lorenzo called early. He wanted to set a time for meeting with Father, but I could not bring myself to do it. I was so terrified of Father. I was practically crying, and with a knot in my throat, I advised Lorenzo, "Please do not come; He will get mad at all of us—your dad, you, and me." He assured me that did not matter; he was already expecting Father to get mad so why was I acting like this?" His tone changed, and with a firm voice, he asked me one last time, "Are you sure you don't want to do this?" "We had it all planned out; I wanted to do this right for both of us." "Are you sure about your final decision?" Nervously, I replied, "I am sorry, but please, no, do not come." Lorenzo was a genuine gentleman; I let him walk away.

After I changed my mind about the meeting with my parents, Lorenzo was different; he was more distant. He did not want to see me, he started to avoid me, and things were never the same. I missed Lorenzo's conversations so I went to his house every chance I got. Mother noticed and started taking me to town instead of Camila. I did not want to go, but Father made me because he too noticed I was hanging around Lorenzo frequently and worried I would have the same fate as Magdalena and elope. He would not be a part of that.

Father tried to make my experience a better one for he knew I was hurting. So he made my time worthwhile, and it was not all that bad. He showed me how our budget had to match our groceries. At first, I hated going shopping, but I learned how to select fruits and vegetables, weigh them, and compared prices in order to get the better bargain. I found it useful and felt included for once. I missed being around Lorenzo and Mirna, my new best friend, but it was for the better that I was not around him anymore. This helped me get over his inattention toward me. I learned to accept his rejection; however, I developed resentment toward him. I guess I broke his heart, or his ego, and he assumed I did not feel the same toward him. The truth was I was not ready to disappoint my father just months after Magdalena's elopement. He and Mother were miserable already, but in public they had to appear normal. "You know, it is always about keeping good appearances, right?" I knew they were going through a tough time. They did not sleep the day Magdalena left, and they argued with each other. It was impossible to accept that their thirteen-year-old daughter was pregnant; she was a child herself.

About a year later, a guy by the name of Franco started making appearances at my parents' house. Franco was a friend to three of my brothers and pretty soon became a family friend. Franco was funny and not bad-looking either, but I had been disappointed before and was not willing to open my heart to someone else. Our conversations started as small talk; then I found myself looking forward to his visits, as did he. Later, Franco became my boyfriend, and I was going to marry him two years into our relationship, but things never happen as we plan, do they?

I had started to work at a nearby burger place called Mom's and Pop's Burgers. I was working the entire week, except Sundays, from eight in the morning to ten in the evening. They were long hours, but I was earning $150 every two weeks, of which I would give Father fifty dollars for taking me to work. You see, Father never taught us girls how to drive; he taught the boys though. So I made a point of telling him I was ready for work about fifteen minutes before my actual time because I knew it was going to be a fiesta, or quite the event getting me there. Father was a hard worker even at home; he always had something to do, so his time was valuable. It never failed that when we pulled out of the driveway at home a bunch of cars would pass at the same time, or so it seemed to Father. As we waited, he scratched his head and said anxiously, "Ah, pero como se les ocurre salir a todos al mismo tiempo que yo hombre." ("Gees, why does everyone seem to leave their homes at the same time I do?") He would shout all the way to work. Like I said, it was a fiesta, but I love my father dearly. He was always there when I needed him.

I knew at some point I had to learn how to drive to work, so in a desperate attempt, I convinced my younger brother Santiago (Chago) to teach me. He was reluctant at first, but then he said okay if I did not tell Father. I agreed, and we headed out for our first and only driving lesson. Two of my other brothers wanted to tag along so, we took them with us, but that was a huge mistake. I was in the driver's seat, Santiago sat next to me showing me what to do, and Ernesto and Benjamin were in the back seat, unbuckled, observing their big sister.

Of course, Father would not know all this was going on unless the car ended up with dents. I was so excited; fear never crossed my mind. It should have though. Father's car was perfect for learning how to drive. The car was a long, big, light yellow to green, four-door sedan that had withstood a lot of accidents. I remember that day clearly. I considered Chago my bravest brother, because he knew how to drive. Father had taught him. Mind you, he was three years younger than me, which made him about twelve at that time. "Oh my gosh, what was I thinking?" Unfortunately, for Ernesto and Benjamin, who decided to tag along, the adventure was not a pleasing one.

We drove around the neighborhood. Chago told me, my turning technique needed a lot of improvement. As we were approaching the turn to our house, Chago started shouting for me to turn quickly and brake. Él gritó, "Comienza a girar y frenar, ya frena, no, no, cuidado!" ("Start turning and braking, slam the brakes, no, no, watch out!") Then we heard a loud bang; we had hit a pole, and Father's billy goat flew. Everyone ended up in the front seat—seat belts were not enforced back then. As soon as, we found out that Father's billy goat and all of us were safe, we started giggling. We giggled until we could not giggle anymore; our tummies hurt from all the laughing. Chago said I could have killed us and asked why I didn't turn or brake in time. "¿Por qué no me escuchaste cuando te lo dije?" ("Why didn't you listen to me when I told you?") "Eh, you dumb or what?" I said, "You did not teach me that!" We continued to laugh about this for days; luckily we did not get hurt. God was definitely watching over us that day.

I do not think Chago tried teaching me after that incident. If I was ever going to learn how to drive, I needed to do it another way. I made it a goal to save enough money to buy my own car; then, all I would need was a person to teach me. Franco offered to teach me how to drive so I eagerly agreed. He was more than willing to teach me in the maroon four-door Chrysler Cordoba I had purchased. By the time I knew how to drive, I had two cars: the maroon Chrysler Cordoba and the fancy black Regal. I learned to drive at the ripe age of eighteen, a few days before my nineteenth birthday, but I learned and felt accomplished. Franco did not mind teaching me because he was able to drive my car; he loved the car so much that he repainted it for me. It looked amazing! From that time on, I had a lot of men ask me if I was willing to sell my car, but my response was always no. By this time, Franco and I were boyfriend and girlfriend. He came around almost every day and stayed nearly all day at my house. Franco stopped by at eight o'clock or earlier on Sunday mornings to wake us up to go to church, trying not to make too much noise because my sister Emma and her husband, Diego, were in the next room. (We were in one big room separated by a curtain that mimicked a wall.) I would question my parents' behavior toward Franco because they did not seem to mind him being around all the time. They never questioned his behavior. Father did not mind him because he helped convince my younger brothers to go to church. In fact, Franco convinced everyone to go to church. After church, we sometimes went grocery shopping for the family. Of course, I would pay because neither Franco nor my brothers had a job. I occasionally asked Franco if he was going to work, but he said not until his family went up north. He was a migrant worker so it was seasonal work.

A year after working at Mom's and Pop's Burgers, I was offered a job at Crystal's, a chicken place. The pay was more per hour, the hours were flexible, and there was less responsibility, so I took the job. At Mom's and Pop's Burgers, I was operating as a cashier, a cook, and a waitress; I had more responsibility and more hours to work for less pay, but we made the best burgers in town. Franco started speaking about marriage, but I questioned his thinking because he had no job. I asked, "Where would we live?" "You have no job, and I cannot marry or be with you until we have somewhere to live; I will not live with your family." His family was awesome, but I was not going to add another mouth to feed to their table.

So he said that he would go up north, save money, and build our home. I said, "Okay, that sounds like a plan." Never did I assume that it was in the very near future.

Like any couple in their teenage years, we had occasional disagreements here and there, but this one specific argument would be unforgettable. This argument created distrust among sisters, shifted my sense of safety and security, and impacted my life tremendously at so many levels. I cannot recall the argument Franco and I had, but what ensued afterward was completely absurd. He had taken off, quite upset. I think someone told him something about me, so it may have stemmed from jealousy; however, I am not 100 percent sure that was the origin of our fight. Franco was so upset that he took the small teddy bear he had given me. I thought, How could he? I ran inside the house crying.

I was looking in the mirror in the living room, wiping away my tears, when someone snuck up behind me. It was Diego, my brother-in-law. He asked with concern, "What happened?" I said, "Nothing, Franco and I had an argument and he took my bear." "No nesesitas a Franco, aqui estoy yo; yo si te quiero, nos podemos ir a otro lugar!" ("You don't need Franco, I am here, and I love you we can leave to another place.") I said, "Hold up, what, no, no, you are with my sister; you are my brother-in-law." "What is the matter with you; You are out of your mind!" Estas loco! ("Your crazy!") He tried to calm me down, for I was nearly shouting. Then he said, "Emma esta dormida, shh, la vas a despertar." ("Emma is asleep, shh you are going to wake her up.") I shouted back, "Y qué, pues que sepa, que tiene un sinverguenza!" ("So what, she needs to know she has a shameless man!") I ran out of there crying uncontrollably. I could not believe this man. He was family.

I did not know what to do exactly or who to tell. Emma had tried to harm herself just a couple months earlier; She was already heartbroken and had consumed a full bottle of aspirin and/or Tylenol. I could not bring myself to tell her this about Diego. I quickly called Franco, even though he was upset with me, and told him what had happened after we fought. He arrived in a fury and wanted to speak with Diego. I told him no. "My sister does not know, and you know how fragile she is right now; Please do not make a scene." It took a long time to calm down Franco, but he eventually asked me what I was going to do. I said, "I don't know what to do; all my options are restricted in some way." I was scared. That night I went to another room since only a curtain separated my room from Diego and Emma's room. I did not feel safe sleeping in my room after his assertion.

Later that night, Diego appeared outside my window, knocking and whispering my name. "Oye, Julieta, despirta; Soy Diego quiero hablar contigo, tenemos que hablar." ("Hey, Julieta, wake up its me Diego I want to speak with you, we have to talk.") I said, "What the hell! Todavia sigues, pues que te pasa, no estas pensando, voy a gritar si no te vas, bête dejame en paz!" ("What is the matter with you? You still at it, what are you thinking, I am going to scream leave me the hell alone!") After his attempt to continue this ridiculous affair, I got in my car and headed toward Magdalena's house, crying uncontrollably. I explained the whole situation to Magdalena, and she told me I could stay with her as long as I needed, but I had to speak with Father and Mother. I agreed to her request.

The next day I went home to tell Mother what Diego had said and why I had slept at Magdalena's house. Mother did not seem shocked and told me just to ignore him and not to tell my sister. "No le hagas caso, y no le vayas a decir a tú Hermana!" ("Don't tell your sister and don't pay any attention to him!") I said, "What, that is it?" You are not going to do anything about it?" Mother did not answer, so I told her I was going back to Magdalena's house, and if Father asked, she would have to explain everything to him. She agreed to tell Father, but she did not.

That same day after work Father came by Magdalena's house, upset. He yelled at me, "Que te crees tú dormindo, aqui y alla, esta no es tú casa, por qué estas aqui, tú tienes casa!" Angrily, he was asking why I had been at Magdalena's house if I had my own house, and he said I had to return home. I furiously stated, "I told Mother what happened; didn't she tell you?" Me gritó de nuevo, "Tú madre no me ha dicho nada; Que esta pasando?" ("Your mother has not told me anything, what is happening?") I told him what Diego had said and done by my window so I had no choice but to find a safe place. He was in disbelief but insisted I return home. "La casa es más tuya que de ellos." Tienes que irte para tú casa, el que se va es el, y si tú Hermana lo quiere seguir pues que lo siga, o se quede, pero tú te me vas ahorita para la casa!" ("The house is more yours than theirs, you need to return home, the one who needs to leave is he, but if your sister wants to leave with him she can, but you go to your house now!") So I gathered my clothes and went back home.

Father was yelling at Mother. "Mujer, ¿por qué no me dijiste sobre Diego, por qué?" "¡Hiciste mal al no decirme!" ("Woman, why didn't you tell me about Diego, why, you did wrong in not telling me?") Father called Diego and Emma out of their room and took them for a drive; Father did not want to discuss anything in front of everyone at the house. After their meeting, Diego and Emma gathered their clothes and left. I felt terrible. Emma blamed me and my sister Alma, claiming that we were always flirting with him. "What the heck!" That had never crossed my mind. That was absurd. Emma did not believe my story, and of course, Diego denied it all. I was hurt by her false accusations.

Franco was delighted that Diego had left the house, and so was I, but things felt different. I think Mother was upset with me for having caused such commotion. Even though she never said it, I don't think she believed me, but I was glad Father believed me and took my side. It was true, and I did not think it was fair for me to move out. I lamented saying anything. I missed Emma, but she was convinced he was telling her the truth. She left with him. She loved him.

I don't know if the situation with Diego made Franco a bit uncomfortable, but he acted fast on our marriage plans. A couple weeks later, Franco called me and asked if I could stay at his trailer since he and his family were going up north to work and needed someone to house-sit for them. I chuckled and said, "Father would not allow it." However, I was wrong. Father did allow it. He agreed only because Franco would be away. He mumbled that with Franco leaving, there would be no danger of me getting pregnant. I had no idea until the day Franco was leaving that he had begun building his house that same year. Franco told me he had a surprise for me, so we got into my Cordoba and headed toward his house. Then I saw it, the house he had been building for us. It was a small wooden-frame home with three walls up, adjacent to his parents' trailer. It still needed the sheetrock, plywood, and ceiling/roof, but it was almost complete. I was speechless, I asked, " How did you do this; You weren't working, were you?" He claimed he had been doing odd jobs here and there, which included mowing yards and fixing cars. Wow! I was shocked. I guess this is happening, I thought. He reassured me that we were going to happen and soon. I was shitting bricks now; I was going to be married soon. I finally accepted the idea that I was going to be Franco's wife the rest of my life.

A few days later, I took my bags and moved into Franco's trailer. The reality of my situation finally hit me. I was going to get married probably by the end of the year; I cannot say I was excited because I did not know he was building a home in the first place. Everything was still a shock to me, but why if we had been a couple for almost two years? My family knew we were going to be married at some point because our relationship was unfolding. It had been a long and serious one. Hell, everyone expected us to be married already, but I was just not feeling it.

While Franco was away, I had applied and got hired full-time with benefits at the local hospital nearby. It was during this time alone that my brother Ernesto arrived with Diego. I could not believe it, the nerve of Diego to continue with this idea that we could be happy together. I started yelling at my brother. "Why did you bring him here; Why would you?" He shouted from the car, "He gave me five dollars

Sister; I am sorry, but I needed the money!" I asked Diego to return to the car or I would call the cops, and I ran to get my phone. So he left. I was truly agitated that he continued to harass me about his feelings. Unbelievable. I could not sleep well after that day, so I had my friend Lila stay with me for the remaining time.

With Lila as a roommate, we started going out to dances. I loved to dance. I did not see anything wrong with going out as long as I did not lead anyone on or lie about my status, "soon to be married." Lila and I went out about twice a month. We went to weddings, fifteenth birthdays, and other parties; we were having so much fun. Franco knew I was going out to dances but did not seem to mind since it was only dancing. When going out, I made it a point to never give out my name or number to anyone.

What is love? What is it like to fall deeply in love with someone? Does it cause you to do things you never thought you would, such as lie or cheat? Is there really the feeling of butterflies in your stomach? I don't know. You be the judge.

There was a guy who managed to get my full attention despite my refusal to acknowledge his presence over and over again. Jacobo was a tall, thin guy with shiny black hair. He had an attractive mustache, with dimples, and he was funny. He was always smiling in the halls of the hospital, saying good morning to everyone who passed by. He asked me out every chance he had. He was quite the persistent guy. He was determined to go out with me. Jacobo found out that his friend Rodrigo was a family friend of ours, so he used Rodrigo to meet me. Jacobo told Rodrigo, "All I know is I am going to marry Julieta." The statement shocked Rodrigo, and he quickly replied, "This guy, nombre su papa te mata si te le acercas a sus hijas." ("Her father will kill you if you get near his daughters.") Jacobo chuckled and said, "Vamos a ver." ("You will see.") "She is going to be my wife." He worked in the maintenance department, which involved painting and remodeling the halls of the hospital and patient rooms. Whenever Jacobo saw or heard me coming out of a room, he stopped working and stood in the hall, just to watch me walk by. He always smiled back at me. I thought, What is up with that dude; He never works.

I was busy and not interested, so his behavior went on for a while. Then one day Rodrigo came up to me and insisted I meet his friend. So he took me to the end of the hall and said, "Julieta, this is Jacobo; Jacobo, this is Julieta." I realized this was the guy who was always standing by the wall with a smirk on his face and thought, "Oh no." We shook hands, and he smiled. "It is my pleasure, ma'am, to finally meet you. I was thinking about tackling you the next time you passed by so you would notice me." It was funny, and I chuckled. I quickly and anxiously replied, "Well, I've got to get back to work; Nice meeting you, Jacobo." "See you around." I had a busy job. Mind you, I had to answer all the patient call lights, pass out water, bathe, walk, and feed patients on the medical floor. So standing around was not an option for me. I walked numerous times through those halls, too busy and engaged to notice anyone.

Chapter 10

PERSISTENCE PAYS OFF

As I was walking to the hospital cafeteria, Jacobo creeped up behind me and asked, "Can I join you; Remember me; I am the one you try so hard to ignore on a daily basis." He asked if I wanted to go out with him, and I said no again. "I'm sorry; I'm engaged." He calmly replied with confidence, "You cannot be engaged because you are going to marry me!" With a confused look, I smiled and walked away; it was as if he didn't hear me at all. Jacobo asked me out on numerous occasions, and I kept saying no. He said he did not know how to dance, so I was completely turned off by that response. He must have asked at least ten times if I wanted to go out with him, and all ten times I said no.

A couple days went by before I noticed Jacobo was not around as much. Then one day, I came out of a patient's room with a handful of dirty linen to throw in the biohazard cart, and the cart was nowhere around. I sighed and started to walk toward the dirty linen room, and suddenly who shows up but Jacobo. He went to the linen room, put a yellow biohazard bag on the linen cart, and started rolling it my way. He cried out, "Hold on, Jacobo to the rescue!" Obviously, he had to have observed me numerous times, in order to prepare the bag the right way on his first try. I admit I was impressed. I smiled and thanked him and walked away. As I walked away, I turned back and, yes, he was still standing there with a great big smile. I thought, "Wow, this guy does not give up." Later that day, he waited for me to have lunch and requested that I join him. I politely said I only had thirty minutes and had to get back to the floor; they needed me. He stated, "They can handle the ward without you for half an hour; Come on." I smiled, got my food, and started walking back to the medical floor. Of course, he followed and walked with me.

As we were walking side by side, I turned to answer his questions. I could not help notice a big red mark on his neck. I asked, quite insulted, "What happened to your neck?" He got nervous, and his face became flushed. He said he had been checking the oil and the oil apparatus burned him. I did not believe that lame story and started walking faster, heatedly, toward the floor. He was quick to defend his case, smirking, "Should you be jealous? You are engaged, right?" Then I questioned my stance. "Was I jealous?" If yes, why? I felt terrible being cheated on by someone who was not even my boyfriend. I guess this was the first time I questioned my love for Franco. Could I feel love for someone else like Jacobo? I knew I had to find out if my love for Franco was true or if our relationship had become a routine or an expectation that everyone contributed to. After all, Franco was always around my house twelve hours a day, every day.

I thought maybe I had gotten used to him. To avoid any feelings of guilt, I had to break up with Franco and see what that would do to our feelings and us.

I tried to explain my situation to Franco in a letter but made sure to inform him that I had to end our engagement. I started feeling guilty about the feelings I was having for Jacobo. The fact that I felt uneasy or nervous when running into him was clearly confusing me. Maybe I liked the attention Jacobo was giving me. I sent Franco the breakup letter—the breakup letter that forever changed our lives.

Only a couple days had gone by since I had mailed the letter to Franco, so the last thing I expected was him showing up at my employment. This was definitely unexpected. I was not prepared to see him, and I nearly fainted. I was, first of all, surprised because I did not recognize him. He called my name. "Julieta, did you not see me?" I said, "What...what are you doing here?" He had been in Wisconsin just a couple days ago. With his voice half cracked, he asked, "What is happening to you; You said you met someone else?" I said I may have started feeling something toward someone else, and if I was capable of those feelings, I should not lie to you about it while we were still engaged. Franco started fidgeting and popping his fingers; then he replied, "Lo que me quieres decir es que ya no te cientes igual como para casarnos, verdad?" ("What you want to say is you do not have the same feelings for me to marry me, right?") I replied, "Estoy confundida y nesesito darme cuenta antes de cometer un error, disculpame." ("No I am just confused about our situation and need to make sure we are not making a mistake. I am sorry.") Suddenly he turned and grabbed my shoulders, looked straight into my eyes, and moved forward to kiss me. I turned away as he kissed my cheek and whispered, "Pero yo te amo, Julieta, nadie te va querer como yo." He said he loved me, and no one else was going to love me as he did. I could see the desperation in his eyes and wanted so much to comfort him, but it did not feel right to stay any longer. I pulled back, struggling to get out of his tight hold, and said I was sorry. Then I started to walk to my car.

I went to get my things from his family's trailer. Since he had returned, I could not and did not want to stay there anymore. I quickly warned my friend Lila that we had to move out, so she went to gather her clothes and we left. A couple days later he started asking for me at my father's house. He asked my brothers where he could find me, but they refused to tell him. I had given my brothers specific instructions not to say anything about my whereabouts. Franco knew he could bribe someone for information, and yep, he gave Ernesto some dough and he let the cat out of the bag. He told him that I was staying with Magdalena. As soon as he found out, he hurried over to find me.

Unfortunately, my sister was not home. I heard a knock. Franco was knocking frantically. I shouted, "Hold on, I am coming." Then I saw him. He had an awkward grin on his face and said to me, "¿Pensaste que no podría encontrarte verdad?" ("You thought I was not going to find you, right?") I stood in complete shock. No one was home; what was I supposed to do? He asked politely, "Are you going to let me in?" I said, "Why do you want to come in, Que quieres?"

("What do you want?") His tone changed. "Nadamas quiero hablar abre la puerta." ("I only want to talk, open the door.") My gut told me not to open the door, but my heart felt sorry for him, so I let him in.

He walked in, slowly looked around, and asked, "Magdalena is not home, is she?" I said, "No, but she is on her way; I called her." He knew I was lying. I asked if he was hungry. Don't know why, force of habit, I guess, I used to cook for him at Father's house. He said no. He just wanted to see and speak with me. I had started cooking when I felt him behind me. He grabbed my waist and whispered, "I miss you, Julieta." I quickly turned with the hot pan in my hands, nearly burning him, and pushed him away. "What are you doing?" He said, "Why did you break up with me; We were almost there." I replied, "I told you already, and I think it's best you leave now." As soon as I put the pan down he walked toward me. He pulled me to him and attempted to kiss me again. I tried pulling away, but he was too strong. Then he grew furious and shouted, "No te reirás de mí!" ("You will not laugh at me!") Then he slapped me across my face and walked out. I stood still for awhile, in shock, grabbed my burning face then ran to lock the door. I was shaking in fear and called Magdalena right away to tell her what had happened with Franco. She was ready to call the cops, but I convinced her otherwise. That was a huge mistake because the following events occurred.

Later that same day, I went out to get some groceries and noticed I was being followed; it looked like Franco's car. It was Franco! He started honking repeatedly and flashing his lights. He wanted me to stop. I yelled, "Hell no, I am not going to stop after your assault on me today!" Since, I did not stop, I thought he was going to give up; However, he lined up his car next to mine and continued yelling at me to stop. I shouted, "I am not going to stop!" He sped up and drove into the lane in front of me and slammed on his brakes. I steered the wheel to the far left to avoid crashing into him. Luckily there were no cars coming in the other lane. I ended up sideswiping his car, which caused both our cars to collide. With my car still swerving, I slammed on the brakes. I could not believe what was going on. "Was he okay," I wondered. I looked back and saw that he was walking toward my car. I quickly reversed and sped away. I was too frightened to wait for him. I headed frantically to Magdalena's house, crying uncontrollably. Magdalena was calling the cops when Franco arrived. She ran out with her hands up in the air, shouting, "Será mejor que te largues" de aquí; ¡No te metas conmigo, cobarde!" ("You'd better get the hell out of here; you do not mess with me, you coward!")

Magdalena hugged me and reassured me that I was safe. I was so scared I forgot to check the car. I went outside, went around the Cordoba, and noticed a small dent with the paint removed on the right side; other than that scratch the car was fine. I could not believe what had happened. I began to wonder if the thought of killing me had crossed his mind. It sure felt like he was trying to. I was grateful for Magdalena. She was so nurturing, and I loved her for being there for me each and every time I ran into trouble. After that incident, Franco pretty much stayed away from us. I was hoping that would be the last time I had to deal with a life-and-death situation. It was not.

Chapter 11

WHERE DID YOU COME FROM?

The summer before my senior year in high school was the most frustrating and dreadful time of my life. Graduating was supposed to be the most exciting time of a senior's life—the prom, the ring, the pictures, the yearbook, the lettermen, the feeling of owning the school that final year. Unfortunately, it was the worst year of my entire life, or at least it seemed that way at the time.

Kelly was an entering freshman, but she looked much older than fifteen. Kelly, my nightmare and daytime rival, was a girl who appeared out of nowhere my senior year. She had not been in our high school before. It was during Summer when Kelly and I first met. My sister Camila and I routinely went to the nearby store on foot; it was our daily routine, and sometimes we went more than once a day. As we were walking into the store, my neighbor Roland was hugging a short girl, which, I assumed was his girlfriend. I could not really see her, but her hair was a darker blond. He waved at us, and as he was smiling, she pushed him away and started walking furiously toward us. Mientras caminaba, ella me gritaba, ""¿Qué, pinche puta, que quieres, quién te llamó?" ("What, bitch, what do you want, who called you?") I said, "Did you not see *he* waved at me, not the other way around, and besides he is my neighbor, nothing else." Just as I finished saying that, her hands reached for my hair, and she pulled me clear down her knees. I immediately started kicking, or tried, but my long, narrow blue-jean skirt would not allow me to kick. I grabbed her hands as I fell back. Camila threw a Coke bottle at Kelly and ran to the phone booth to call for help; However, Kelly's friend Katherine was guarding the phone and pushed her away. Roland started yelling at Kelly to stop because the cops were coming. That was not true, but it was only then that Kelly stopped kicking me and started running off. She looked back angrily and shouted, "Stay away from my boyfriend!" Everything happened so fast we didn't know what went wrong. Camila ran to me and worriedly asked, "Are you okay?" Her voice cracked; she was practically crying. I replied yeah and asked, "Do you know who she is?" My sister said, "No, I have never seen her around here before." By this time the store manager had found out what was going on and asked us if we were okay. We both said, "Yes, thank you," and he went back inside to attend to customers.

As we headed home, we cautiously scanned the streets for Kelly and her friend. The moment we walked into our driveway, we both sighed, teared up, and looked at each other for a while. There was mutual silence, and then laughter broke out. We asked eachother, "What the hell happened Sister?" Camila asked me, "What did you do, Julieta?" I replied, "I can ask you the same question, Camila; I do not know why she freaked out like that and attacked us." "She must have gotten jealous that Roland waved our way." "Talk about unresolved issues."

After that incident, we rarely went out on foot to the store. That was both sad and upsetting because those girls took away part of our freedom and sense of security. Bullies, I hated them! What makes someone that angry, that jealous, and that sick? I hoped and prayed I would not run into those girls ever again, unfortunately, I did.

The long-awaited first day of my senior year arrived; I was thrilled! I was closer to graduating. A couple weeks had passed, and I was sitting with my small group of friends when I saw Kelly walk by. I thought, "No, it couldn't be—not here, not her, not again, not my senior year!" She was the last person I wanted to see. She was a freshman but she looked much older than a high school student. She did not see me, but I was terrified, my heart started racing, my hands started sweating, and my face started flushing.

After that day, I was much too careful not to hang around the areas where she hung out. Then the unthinkable happened. As routinely happened when the bell rang, everyone walked to class in the crowded hallways. Kelly and I were walking side by side. She remembered me and abruptly stopped. She pushed me, which made me almost fall over a couple students to my right, and started cussing. ¿Qué estás mirando pendeja? ("What are you looking at, fucking bitch?") I replied, "I do not even know you; What is your problem?" "I am not going to fight you." "What do you want?" By this time, students had already started to form a circle, screaming, "Fight, fight, fight!" I said, "No, I will not fight" and squeezed through the crowd to the bathroom. Of course, Kelly followed me. She was trying to prevent me from going into the bathroom by pulling my shirt. I guess she liked the attention. Once inside the bathroom, *shouting and lifting her fists*, she says, "Andale vamos pinche puta?" ("Come on, fucking bitch!") I turned and walked into the bathroom stall and locked it. She kept banging on the bathroom door, saying, "Come on, bitch, I want to fight." I just told her, "You have problems and they are not with me, so leave me alone." The tardy bell rang, and she finally left, kicking the door one last time and yelling that I better watch my back.

I was too scared to move, so I waited a bit longer before leaving the bathroom. Yes, she scared me a lot, but I was not about to let her see what she was doing to me. I figured she was more upset that she did not get to punch me. I assured myself and headed back to class. I was late. For that whole year, I hated to go to school for the fear of running into Kelly. I hated her for being such an ugly person to me, and I hated my life because I let her take away from what should have been a great senior year. I honestly felt there was nothing else to love, but not once did I think about ending my life because of her. I was not about to give her the power of controlling me. She was not going to win! It was not that the thought never crossed my mind, but because I was a Catholic, suicide was not a solution. God does not forgive taking your own life, and if God is in your life, you should not have those thoughts.

As you probably have noticed by now, I've had my share of bullies, and today they are still present in my life. Harming yourself is never the answer out of any problem.

As dreadful, hopeless, and frustrating your life gets, you have to face the bully and tell someone. If that person does not help you, tell someone else. Bullying is a behavior that should never be accepted or laughed at. Ask someone for help—your family, a friend, counselor, teacher, or coworker—but do not take your life!

People say life prepares us for the challenges we encounter. The truth is you will never be prepared. Expect to be disappointed sometime in your life, and maybe it will not tear you down as much. Life happens. Expect struggles, expect to fail, but do not give up, head up. Every day is a new day and a day to start all over again. Every little girl dreams of having her own fairy tale—meeting a knight in shining armor and living happily ever after. The truth is your knight does not come on a white horse unless you live in Texas, where it might happen. We need to communicate the real challenges going on in our lives, not withholding the bad moments. We need to address the critical issues that our society has minimized, which include bullying and domestic violence. If my life's triumphs and failures can help one person, my purpose in writing this book has been achieved.

My life with Jacobo took on a new beginning. We had great moments, but unfortunately we had dreadful moments too. We matured together as friends, as a couple, and as new parents, but nothing prepared me for what I was about to experience. We grew apart and learned to hate the best of each other. They say time heals wounds, but the truth is you learn to forgive because if you do not forgive, you will be miserable for the rest of your life. Life is too precious to spend it hating others and regretting the choices you have made. The truth is people do not change when they do not want to. There comes a point in your life when you have to make important decisions, such as reporting your bully, stop being the bully, or leaving an abusive relationship. What will you do? If you do not do anything, who is your decision affecting? We all deserve to be loved. We are all capable of love. Hopefully, you will make the right decision to run the other way if you have to, to tell somebody that someone else is making your life miserable, or to have plenty of good coping mechanisms to deal with your daily stressors and challenges.

In my situation, being raised in the Catholic faith played a substantial role in my life, and it is the only reason I am able to write about it today. Have someone, have something, have purpose, or better yet, have God in your life, and you shall rise much stronger each and every time life brings you challenges. Catholic principles were the foundation of our family's way of life and functioned well until drugs, alcohol, jealousy, and physical abuse consumed a man I once grew to love. Unfortunately, life can be unpleasant. Whether it is divorce or separation versus being left alone, choose the one decision that leaves you breathing.